THE JERSEY

IT'S MAGIC!

Adapted by Jay Sinclair
Based on the series created by Gordon Korman

New York

Copyright © 2000 by Disney Enterprises, Inc.

All rights reserved. No part of this book may be reproduced
or transmitted in any form or by any means, electronic or
mechanical, including photocopying, recording, or by any
information storage and retrieval system, without written
permission from the publisher. For information address
Disney Press, 114 Fifth Avenue, New York, New York 10011-5690

Printed in the United States of America.

First edition
1 3 5 7 9 10 8 6 4 2

Library of Congress Catalog Card Number: 00-100171

ISBN 0-7868-4261-X
For more Disney Press fun, visit www.disneybooks.com

CONTENTS

CHAPTER ONE

TACKLED BY THE TRASH

"Okay, Morgan, curb jump draw. Elliott, half-back fake. 'Slaw, trash-can split on three. Blue thirty-six. Blue thirty-six. Hut hut hut!"

Nick Lighter smiled broadly as he rolled back on his in-line skates and prepared to pass the football to one of his three best pals—Elliott Rifkin, Coleman "the 'Slaw" Galloway, and Nick's cousin, Morgan.

There was nothing in the world that Nick loved doing more than playing football. And whenever he and his pals played, Nick made sure he was the quarterback, just like his all-time favorite player, San Francisco 49ers quarterback Steve Young.

Nick liked being the quarterback because it meant he called the shots. And when it came to quarterbacks, Steve Young was one of the best. Besides being the Superbowl MVP in 1994, he'd been in the Pro Bowl seven times, and he held the NFL record for most consecutive games, in which he threw for three hundred yards.

Nick believed that, like Steve Young, he too was destined for football greatness one day. His very name proved it— Nicholas Farrell Lighter. That made his initials NFL. Just like the National

Football League. Someday, Nick's face would be smiling out at millions of fans from boxes of Wheaties. Kids would be wearing Nick Lighter sneakers, and buying magazines with his picture on the cover. Nick would be a huge sports hero, with the endorsement deals to prove it!

To ensure his future, Nick studied every play he saw on TV and tried to repeat it whenever he played in-line skate street football with his friends. In fact, in some ways, Nick believed that trying to catch a ball while on blades was tougher than real football. After all, the only thing real football players had to watch out for were opposing players wanting to tackle them. But having to maneuver around parked cars, garden sprinklers, and trash cans while keeping his balance on wheels often made it difficult for Nick to call plays the way a real quarterback might. Nick accepted the challenge—and the danger. It was all part of being the ultimate football fan, which Nick definitely was!

Right now, Nick had to focus on the in-line blade challenge at hand. The young quarterback reached his arm back as though he were going to throw the football to his cousin, Morgan, who was also playing today. But instead of releasing the ball, he reached out his arm and pretended to hand the ball off to one of his two best friends, Elliott. *Fake-out!*

Elliott reached for the ball, but Nick held tight. *Another fake-out!* Finally, Nick's other best friend, Coleman, skated out in front of Elliott, slipped between two metal trash cans, and reached up his hands. He was ready to receive Nick's pass.

Nick released the ball and sent it spiraling through the air.

"I got it! I got it!" Coleman cried out.

But Morgan had other ideas. With a grin, she turned around and bladed at top speed toward the trash cans. She launched herself in the air, right between Coleman and the cans.

"Get out of here!" Coleman shouted to her. "It's my ball!"

Morgan pretended not to hear Coleman's cries as she leaped up into the air. She reached her arms up high above her head and grabbed the ball before Coleman could even get near it. Then she bent her knees and made a perfect landing on the sidewalk, with the ball tucked firmly under her arm.

"Impossible!" Elliott exclaimed, as he rode his board over toward Morgan.

"Awesome!" Nick agreed. His cousin sure had some great moves!

Coleman, however, was not as impressed. But before he could add his thoughts . . . *CRASH!* Coleman collided with the two trash cans. The cans tipped over. Coleman's in-line skate wheel slid over some slimy stuff, and he landed in a pile of garbage.

"Interception!" Elliott called out, as he hopped off his skateboard and went to help lift his friend from the mound of smelly trash.

"Aargh!" Coleman exclaimed. He was more angry than embarrassed. "That was *my* ball, Morgan! I had it all the way."

Morgan pulled off her helmet triumphantly and wiped her long reddish-brown hair from her face. Then she looked down and inspected her hands.

"Didn't even break a nail," she joked, as she reached down into the pile of garbage and helped Coleman to his feet.

Nick chuckled. He knew that his cousin was the last girl to be concerned with something like a broken nail. Morgan was anything but a girly-girl.

Coleman, however, was not amused by Morgan's sense of humor. "Maybe that's how you do things in Chicago, but around here, you stick to the play," he huffed angrily at Morgan.

Morgan turned away for just a second. She felt as though maybe she'd gone too far. After all, she and her mom had only moved to this St. Louis suburb a few days ago from their home in Chicago. Her cousin Nick and his friends were the only kids she'd hung out with since she'd arrived. Not that that was a bad thing or anything.

The truth was, Elliott and Coleman were really cool guys in their own way. Elliott might be a little cautious sometimes, but that was just because he was so clever. He was able to analyze just about any situation and figure out the dangers and the best plan of action. He was the one who kept a very exact record of all the plays that occurred during Monday Night Football games.

And Coleman was *so* smart and funny. He got straight A's but liked to joke around about everything—except football, of course. That he took *very* seriously. Which, for that matter, so did Morgan. Elliott and Coleman were great to be around. So maybe getting Coleman mad at her wasn't such a terrific idea.

But then Morgan remembered one of the things her grandfather had always taught her.

TACKLED BY THE TRASH

"'Slaw," she said, using Coleman's nick-
name, "sometimes you gotta make the
play . . ."

". . . or let the play make you." Nick
finished his cousin's thought. He'd once
shared the same conversation with their
grandfather. And although Nick's grandfather had been an ambitious athlete, his
views on sports were a little old-fashioned.
The old man had thought that all football
was about was stuff like teamwork and
practicing. Still, this was one of his
grandfather's witticisms Nick had
always agreed with. It was the daring
players who became league superstars.
And it was the league superstars who
wound up with the nice, fat contracts.

Elliott laughed as Nick finished
Morgan's thought. "Something else you
learned from your grandfather?" he asked

the cousins. Nick and Morgan smiled and gave each other a high five.

But Coleman wasn't giving in just because of some saying Nick and Morgan's grandfather had taught them. He was still plenty angry. He just shook his head, brushed an old banana peel from his leg, and refused to even reply to Morgan and Nick's little football strategy lesson. He glared angrily at Morgan. Morgan turned away and looked to Nick for help.

"Okay, my house, six-fifteen tonight," Nick told Elliott and Coleman, quickly changing the subject.

The three boys huddled together, slapped hands, and then broke.

"Monday Night Football Club rocks!" they shouted together.

Morgan frowned. The mention of the Monday Night Football Club immediately made her feel left out. Nick had started the club before Morgan had ever moved to town, to make sure that he, Elliott, and Coleman shared every single game together. The boys met in Nick's family room every Monday night during football season, drank soda and ate pizza, and watched the game.

Even though Morgan and the guys had played ball, gone skating, and hit the BMX bike trails together almost every day since she'd arrived in town, the MNFC was still an all-male group. And that didn't seem particularly fair to Morgan. After all, she liked to watch football just as much as the guys did. And she knew all the players and their stats every bit as well as Coleman, Nick, and Elliott. Still, when it came to being invited to her cousin's house for his weekly Monday night pizza-and-sports fest, Morgan had been completely left out.

"C'mon, Nick, you said you'd talk to the guys about letting me join the MNFC," she reminded her cousin as Coleman and Elliott rolled off to their homes to do their homework before the game began.

"Relax, you've only been here a few days," Nick replied.

"Exactly," Morgan said. "You're the only people I know."

Nick looked away from Morgan's eyes and fidgeted with the string on his sweatshirt.

"Look, it's not me. . . ." Nick began as the two cousins skated around the corner and up his driveway. "The guys are very picky about who gets in. This has to be handled . . . carefully." He stared straight ahead at the house, avoiding Morgan's doubtful expression. He couldn't actually face his cousin with the truth: not only was she a girl, but she was a girl who might actually be better at sports than he was. And Nick liked being the big cheese in the MNFC.

Morgan scowled as she kicked off her blades. She had a feeling it wasn't the guys who had a problem with her joining the club. She thought it might be Nick who didn't want to let her in. After all, her cousin Nick was the one who had started the MNFC in the first place. Morgan was pretty sure he could persuade his buddies to let her into the club. For some weird reason he didn't seem to want to.

That made Morgan feel kind of sad, and let down by in her cousin. She'd always thought of him as her closest friend, even though up until recently they had lived pretty far from each other. She really hoped the problem wasn't that Nick wanted to keep girls out of the club. That would really have disappointed her. But the truth was, although he'd never treated her any differently from any other friend before, now that they were all in junior high, things were starting to change at school. Being "just friends" with guys was getting more difficult. And maybe Nick felt weird about Morgan's being part of his all-boys night.

Still, there was plenty of time for them to talk about that later. For now, Morgan silently followed her cousin into his house.

CHAPTER TWO

DISAPPOINTED TO THE MAX

When Nick and Morgan wandered into the family room, they found Nick's mom, dad, and sister, Hilary, as well as Morgan's mom (who was Nick's aunt April), all sitting on the couch. They were staring at an old wooden trunk with a big padlock on the front of it. It seemed as though no one was completely ready to open it and find out what was inside. Or maybe they were just waiting for Nick and Morgan to arrive, so the whole family could be together when they did.

"What's that?" Nick asked as he threw down his bookbag and plopped onto the couch beside his dad.

"Your grandpa's old trunk," he replied. "Seems that after two years, Aunt Maybelle finally got around to sending it."

Nick sighed. It was hard to believe that his grandfather had been gone two years already.

"Shall we?" Nick's dad continued, gesturing toward the trunk.

"Why not?" Hilary agreed.

"Sure," Nick's aunt April said excitedly. She seemed curious to find out what was hidden inside her father's trunk.

Nick's dad pulled out a small key from an envelope and cautiously opened the old lock. Then he picked up the curved wooden lid and peered inside. Dust flew into the air when Nick's family peered over the top to see what was inside. Obviously, this trunk had been sealed up for a long time.

As Nick and Morgan could have predicted, the trunk was filled with old, dusty sports memorabilia. Their grandfather had been a huge sports fan. He had loved all sports—soccer, hockey, basketball, baseball, even lacrosse. But football had been his favorite. He'd played football in college, back in the time before football became a huge multimillion dollar business. And even though he'd never gone pro, he'd kept his love of the sport his entire life.

Nick's mom picked up a letter that had been left on top of the trunk. Nick looked over his mom's shoulder. The letter was written in his grandfather's strong, sure, left-handed writing. Nick recognized it from all the birthday cards his grandfather had sent him over the years.

"'To my family,'" Nick's mom read aloud. "'These were the items that defined my life. I hope they enhance yours. Love, Grandpa.'"

"That's it?!" Nick's dad exclaimed with more than a little disappointment. "That's all he had to say?"

Nick's mom turned the letter over. There was a list on the back of the paper. "And a list of who gets what," she said. "That's all."

Nick's dad looked frustrated. He obviously wanted his father to have written something more. But deep down, Nick's dad knew that wasn't his father's style.

"Pop wasn't much of a talker," he said finally.

"Maybe you weren't listening," Nick's aunt April told her older brother softly.

Nick nodded in agreement. "He always talked to me," he told his dad.

"Me, too," Morgan seconded, looking up at her uncle. "Football, baseball, hockey . . . he'd talk all day about that stuff." Morgan's face grew bright as she recalled some of the spirited discussions she and her grandfather once had. The man had been like a walking sports encyclopedia. Morgan had learned so much from him about obscure plays and the great sportsmen in the times before television. The afternoons she'd spent with her grandfather had been some of the best in her life.

Nick's older sister, Hilary, sighed and

looked at her watch. Unlike her brother and cousin, Hilary had little interest in sports. She was more into theater, music, and boys. And this conversation was boring her to tears.

"Excuse me, but can we get this over with?" Hilary asked, stretching her long, lanky legs. 'Melrose Creek' starts in ten minutes."

Morgan laughed. "Relax, I always set the VCR at my house," she assured her older cousin.

Hilary smiled gratefully at Morgan and sat back as her dad pulled an old photo album from the trunk. It's good to have another girl around, Hilary thought.

"That's for you and April," Nick's mom told her husband as she handed him an old, dusty photo album and checked the list.

Nick's dad's face brightened as he looked at his dad's old pictures. The first few pictures were old black-and-white snapshots, from back when Nick's dad and aunt were just kids. One of them showed Nick's dad on his very first baseball team. He couldn't have been more than seven years old. Nick grinned. It was always fun to think of his dad as a little boy.

"That was one of the few times the old man ever put his arm around me," Nick's dad murmured quietly as he looked longingly at the picture of himself.

Nick's aunt April turned the page. There were more pictures of her and her brother at their old home. Then, suddenly, the pictures switched from black-and-white to color, as they became photos of Hilary, Nick, and Morgan playing all sorts of sports together and separately.

Nick's aunt stopped to admire a photograph of Nick and Morgan in their junior soccer league uniforms. "Look at the cousins," she remarked sweetly.

Hilary looked down at the picture and laughed. Nick looked almost the same as he did now, with his thick, dark-brown hair and big brown eyes. But Morgan sure had changed. In the photograph, Morgan's reddish-brown hair was really, really short, as if someone had placed a bowl on her head and cut around it. The style was a far cry from the long straight hair Morgan had now.

"What loser cut your hair like that?" Hilary teased Morgan.

"I did," April told her niece sharply.

Oops. Hilary sat back and didn't say a thing.

Nick's dad reached into the trunk and

began pulling out more sports equipment. There were old sneakers and cleats. A big wooden baseball bat, a football helmet, and a huge silver trophy were tucked off toward the side. Nick's dad lifted the trophy from the trunk.

"'Nineteen Forty-six Division Champs,'" Nick's dad said, reading from the plaque at the base of the statue. "That was when your grandfather threw a seventy-two-yard touchdown pass in the final seconds of the game."

Nick let out a whistle. "That's gotta be some kind of record," he guessed.

"It was. If he hadn't blown his knee out, your grandpa could have gone pro."

Nick's mom looked at the list and pointed to the trophy. "That's for Hilary."

Nick's dad proudly handed the huge metal trophy to his daughter. She took it from him and looked it over from top to bottom and shook it upside down. "Where am I supposed to put this?" Hilary asked her dad with a frown. "It doesn't match anything in my room. It's dirty and hollow."

Nick rolled his eyes. His sister obviously didn't get the significance of the trophy. "Matches your head perfectly," Nick said, goading her.

"Nick!" both of his parents exclaimed at the exact same time.

Morgan reached down into the trunk and pulled out an old, chocolate-brown football. "Yes!" she shouted, tossing the football gently in the air. "I wondered what happened to this. Autographed by the '67 Packers. It's a classic."

Nick reached over and grabbed the football from his cousin's grasp. "That's gotta be mine!" he declared.

Nick's mom looked over at the ball. "That man sure loved football," she said.

Just then, Leonardo, the family's small brown-and-white beagle, began barking wildly at the trunk. The dog had seen something no one else in the family had— an old woolen sweater that was packed away on the side of the trunk had moved— all on its own! It seemed to be trying to escape from the trunk! Leonardo nervously grabbed the sleeve of the old woolen jersey in his mouth and started to tug.

"He liked football almost as much as he hated dogs." Nick's dad laughed. He pulled the sweater sleeve from the dog's jaws. "Down, Leonardo! Get away from there."

Morgan reached her hands over toward the autographed football. "C'mon, Nick," she pleaded. "Let me see it!"

But Nick held on tight to the ball.

"Nick, that belongs to Morgan," Nick's mom told him gently.

Nick's jaw dropped. His grandfather had left the prized autographed football to *Morgan*? That couldn't be right! "Huh? No way!"

Morgan grabbed the football before Nick knew what hit him. "Hah!" she exclaimed triumphantly.

Leonardo barked wildly and tugged harder on the sleeve of the orange-yellow football jersey with blue sleeves. Nick's dad reached over and wrested the sleeve from the dog's mouth.

Hilary lifted the dog in her arms and kissed his fur. "Leonardo, don't touch that thing," she scolded him gently. "That's a good boy."

Nick's mom looked from the jersey to

the letter. "Nick, that jersey is for you," she told her son.

Nick's dad proudly handed his son his father's old football jersey.

Nick took the jersey in his hands. It wasn't like any football jersey he had ever seen. Instead of being thin and soft, like the jerseys modern football players wore, this old shirt was thick and woolen, and very heavy. The shirt itself was orange-yellow, but the sleeves were blue. A big blue letter *H* was sewn onto the middle of the jersey. One of the cuffs had been torn. It also smelled slightly of mothballs. And the jersey was huge—his grandfather had already been in college when he'd worn it. What was Nick supposed to do with this ratty old thing?

"That'll look great on you," Morgan teased, "if you ever grow!"

"Shut up, Morgan," Nick barked back. He looked at the jersey and felt his eyes begin to water. As much as Nick had loved his grandfather, he and the old man had had some pretty heavy arguments about modern football. Nick had thought that his favorite players were the greatest of all time, but his grandfather disagreed. He'd felt that modern football players were spoiled brats who cared more for their bank accounts than for the game itself. He had had no patience for players who spent their time making commercials or lending their names to sneaker companies.

Nick had thought that those arguments were just friendly disagreements—differences between generations. But as he looked over at the football Morgan was carrying, Nick assumed that he had been wrong. His grandfather had obviously been angry at him. Why else would he have left the football to Morgan, and given him some itchy old football jersey? Nick's grandfather had obviously taken those arguments seriously, and now it was too late for Nick to ever apologize.

Frustrated, Nick dropped the jersey and grabbed the autographed Packers football right out of Morgan's arms. Quickly he raced for the door.

"Nick! Give it back!" Morgan shouted as she ran after him.

Nick was so intent on hanging on to the football that he threw the front door open without even noticing that Elliott and Coleman had just stepped up onto the porch. It was six-fifteen, and they were ready for their MNFC pregame pizza.

The door slammed into Coleman. Coleman was thrown off balance, and fell off the side of the porch. He landed right in a bed of petunias. Coleman shook his head in disbelief. This was obviously not his day.

"Hey!" he shouted after Nick. But Nick just blew past him.

"Nick! Quit acting like a jerk!" Morgan screamed.

"The list was wrong!" Nick insisted. "He and I played with this ball. I remember . . ."

Elliott looked from the feuding cousins to Coleman. He sauntered over to the flower bed and extended his hand. "You want help?" Elliott asked.

Coleman rolled his eyes. "Does it look like I need help?" he replied sarcastically, grabbing Elliott's hand and pulling himself up.

Morgan dove for Nick and tried to grab the autographed ball. Nick ducked to the right and avoided her grasp. But he knew that he wasn't going to be able to hold on to that football forever. Especially now that his parents had come out into the front yard.

"Nick!" Nick's dad scolded his son.

"Dad, check that letter again," Nick begged. "Grandpa must've left me the football. Not some jersey I never even saw before."

Nick's dad sighed and shook his head. "That's what the letter said, Nick. The ball is *hers*."

Nick looked at his dad through pleading eyes. But Nick's father's firm expression made it clear. Nick was going to have to give the ball back to Morgan. Still, nobody said he had to do it nicely. He tossed the ball back and stomped past her toward the house.

"Let's go. It's almost kickoff time," Nick said loudly to Elliott and Coleman. He made a point of not looking in Morgan's direction as he headed inside. Coleman and Elliott walked behind him. Morgan tried to follow, but Nick angrily blocked the door. There was no way he was letting Morgan watch the game with the MNFC.

"Oh, I get it," Morgan said. "Now I can't join."

Nick nodded. *"Ping!* That's right. Bob, tell her what she's won," he declared, imitating a game show host. "It's an old worthless football!"

Morgan shook her head. Nick was being ridiculous.

"We're not taking any new members," Nick told Morgan definitively.

"Why not?" Coleman interrupted.

"I know as much about football as you," Morgan told her cousin.

"I'd have to say, that's true," Elliott told Nick.

Nick scowled at Elliott and shook his head angrily. "No way! Not today. Not ever!" he declared.

"Fine!" Morgan replied. "I don't want to hang out here anyway!"

Nick smiled triumphantly as his cousin walked toward her mother's car. That was one battle he had won. But somehow, in his heart of hearts, Nick had a feeling this war wasn't over.

CHAPTER THREE

TOO WEIRD!

By the time the first quarter began, the members of the Monday Night Football Club had all but forgotten about Nick's battle with Morgan. They were in Nick's family room, munching on pizza, downing liters of Coke, and busily awaiting the start of the Kansas City Chiefs–Oakland Raiders game.

As always, while they waited, the guys were busy playing their own game of "family room football." Nick took on the part of quarterback Steve Young. He picked up his football and ran toward the bookshelves.

"Young back to pass," Nick said in his best deep, excited TV-sports-announcer voice. "He sees Rice open over the couch."

Elliott, who was playing the part of *his* favorite pro football star, San Francisco 49ers wide receiver Jerry Rice, leaped up in the air to catch the ball as Nick lobbed it toward him. The ball landed squarely in Elliott's arms as he dove into the couch.

"Touchdown!" Nick cheered. "Let's see that again in slow motion."

Nick took the ball back, and he and Elliott repeated the play. But this time they moved ever so slowly, as though they were being shown on a slow-mo replay on Monday Night Football.

But before the imaginary crowd could

cheer, Nick's dad walked into the family room, holding Nick's grandfather's football jersey.

"Hey, guys," Nick's dad greeted the MNFC. Then he turned and looked sternly at his son. "Nick, this meant a lot to your grandfather. I don't want to find it on the floor again. Got it?"

Nick's dad tossed the old woolen jersey to his son. "Yeah, Dad," Nick said wearily. He was sorry to have been reminded that his grandfather had left him the old football shirt instead of the autographed Packers ball.

"Enjoy the game, boys," Nick's dad said as he left the room.

Nick looked down at the jersey. What had his grandfather been thinking?

"Game time!" Elliott shouted, interrupting Nick's thoughts.

Just then, Coleman took the opportunity to tackle Elliott on the couch. But Elliott wasn't going down without a fight. He picked up a pillow and whacked Coleman in the head.

Nick ignored his friends and studied the jersey for a while. "Actually, this could be a pretty wicked Halloween costume," he muttered as he slipped the jersey over his head. As he stuck his arms through the sleeves, Nick felt a slight tingle in his arms. Man, this old jersey is itchy, he thought, as he scratched at his arm. Well, if he did wear the jersey on Halloween, he might be a little uncomfortable.

Suddenly a flash of light burst through the room. It was as though lightning had struck right in the family room. Coleman and Elliott were too busy watching the game to notice it. But Nick blinked as the light hit his eyes. Before he knew what was happening, Nick's hand and arm turned clear—like plastic. He could see a transparent, bloodlike liquid running through his veins. Strangely, though, Nick wasn't nervous. He didn't even have time to be. In a matter of a few seconds, the light grew brighter as Nick's body grew thinner and thinner . . . until it completely disappeared from the family room.

The next thing Nick knew he was in a big, smelly locker room. There were benches, showers, and lockers—just like the locker room at school. But this wasn't his school gym locker room, or any other place he'd ever been in before. Nothing looked familiar here.

"Coleman? Elliott?" Nick asked nervously as he searched around frantically for a familiar face.

TOO WEIRD!

But Coleman and Elliott were nowhere to be seen. Instead, Nick found himself surrounded by huge hulking football players, all wearing Oakland Raiders football jerseys.

He had gone from watching the game in his family room to hanging out in the locker room with the actual Oakland Raiders. This was too weird! There had to be some logical reason why he was suddenly hundreds of miles from home, in a football locker room that few kids had ever seen before. But as much as Nick wracked his brains trying to think of a reason, he couldn't come up with a thing.

As Nick looked around the Raiders' locker room his eyes landed on a mirror. But instead of his own reflection staring back at him, Nick saw the Raiders' famous defensive back Charles Woodson staring right back at him. Nick blinked, trying to figure out if this was some sort of bizarre dream. But when he opened his eyes again, it was still Charles Woodson's face and hulking muscular body staring back at him from the mirror! Nick moved his thick, powerful, muscle-bound arms. The Charles Woodson in the mirror moved *his* arms as well. Nick kicked one leg. The Charles Woodson reflection kicked *his* leg in exactly the same way. There was no doubt about it. Nick was Charles Woodson!

"AAAAHHH!" Nick screamed. He wasn't sure what to think. Part of him refused to believe that he had suddenly become a completely different person. And not just any person, but a famous professional football player. But the mirror wasn't lying. He really had become Charles

Woodson, who, if you had to be someone else, was a pretty cool guy to be. After all, not only was Woodson one of the greatest defensive backs in the NFL today, he'd won a Heisman Trophy back when he was in college.

Wait until I tell the guys about this one! Nick mused. Then he stopped. How could he tell Elliott and Coleman that he had entered Charles Woodson's body? They'd never believe him. And they would totally razz on him for being out of his mind.

It was all so bizarre and creepy!

Nick moved nervously away from the mirror . . . and backed right into a laundry hamper filled with dirty towels!

The Oakland Raiders laughed harder than they had in months. Woodson wasn't exactly known as the team funnyman, which made his antics seem even more amusing. And his teammates weren't about to let the fun and games end there. One of the giant football players gave the cart a little shove. But a little shove from a big guy can wield a lot of power. Nick went soaring across the floor of the locker room at the speed of a car on the highway. Nick held on to the sides with his suddenly huge hands, and looked frightened. The now hysterical Raiders started throwing towels at him.

As he ducked the flying mounds of white terry cloth, Nick ran his fingers over the Oakland Raiders football jersey that now covered his body. Quickly, he stripped the uniform shirt from his body.

There was another flash of light, just like the one in his living room. By now, the other players had gone back to their lockers and were busy getting ready for the game. They never saw Nick's arm turn clear or his body begin to grow thinner and thinner until finally he disappeared from the locker room completely.

The next thing Nick knew, he was back in his family room. And, he assumed, Charles Woodson was back where *he* belonged.

"Hey, did you guys see that?" Nick asked Coleman and Elliott excitedly.

"See what?" Elliott asked. He threw another pillow at Coleman's head.

"See *what*?!" Nick asked incredulously. "I was sucked into . . . my body stretched and . . ."

Coleman and Elliott looked at Nick as though he were crazy. Then they turned their attention back to the TV. A sports reporter was speaking from the Raiders' locker room.

Charles Woodson was on the screen. He

looked confused as he pulled a white towel from his shoulder.

Nick pointed excitedly at the screen. "Charles Woodson! I was . . . him!" he told the others. He was suddenly too excited to care if his friends teased him.

Coleman shook his head and rolled his eyes. "You're *Young*," he reminded Nick, thinking his pal was talking about their family-room football game. "You're *always* Steve Young."

"Guys, keep it down," Elliott interrupted. "The game's starting."

Nick looked down and touched his arms and legs. They sure felt like his again. But he was certain that he'd been inside Charles Woodson's body for just a few minutes.

It had all started when he put that old football shirt on. . . .

TOO WEIRD!

There was something weird about that jersey. Nick was sure of it. He just didn't know quite what the jersey was capable of doing. The only person who would have known that was his grandfather, and he couldn't ask him. He'd just have to wait and see exactly what the jersey was going to do next.

That thought frightened Nick. But it also excited him, *big time*! After all, he now knew what it felt like to be in a pro football player's body. And that feeling had been kind of cool!

CHAPTER FOUR

RORY'S FURY

Nick didn't pay a whole lot of attention to the game that night. In fact, by the next morning, he couldn't even recall the final score. All he could think about was the jersey, and how he had somehow become Charles Woodson.

"Look, you must have been daydreaming," Elliott assured Nick as the members of the MNFC biked their way to school the next morning. "You were *not* Charles Woodson."

"Yeah," Coleman agreed. "Now shut up and call a play."

Nick nodded in agreement. Elliott had to be right. Elliott was always right. He was smart, logical, and scientific, and he always thought things through.

Still, it had felt awfully real for a daydream.

But Nick decided to let the subject drop. He had a feeling that if he mentioned becoming Charles Woodson one more time, the guys were going to rag on him all day long. So instead, Nick lifted up the football he'd been carrying under his right arm. He steered his bike gingerly with his left hand and rode ahead. Nick grinned. In a lot of ways, bicycle football was even more exciting than in-line skate football. You had to know how to steer with one hand and throw at the same time!

"Okay. Double driveway, slat right. Go!"

Coleman and Elliott sped off down the street. Every now and then Coleman would pop a wheelie just for fun. Nick reached back and let the ball soar out of his hand.

The ball headed straight for Coleman. But just before he could catch the ball, Morgan came riding up out of nowhere. Once again, she blocked Coleman's path, reached up, and grabbed the ball.

"Hey!" Nick shouted at her. "Don't be a jerk just 'cause you're not in my club!"

Elliott looked curiously at Nick. "*Your* club?" he asked.

Nick didn't answer.

Coleman turned to Morgan. "C'mon, Morgan, give it back," he insisted.

"Yeah," Nick agreed. "Quit buggin' me. You're worse than Hilary."

Morgan glared at her cousin. "Hey, at least she's cool," she told him. "Not a selfish jerk like you." Morgan tucked the ball under her arm and rode off at top speed. She turned back and taunted her cousin. "See ya!"

Nick watched as his cousin took off with yet another one of *his* footballs. "She's dead meat!" he told Coleman and Elliott. "Let's go!"

And with that, the chase was on. Nick pedaled as fast as he could, but Morgan had a good head start on him. Still, he stayed close behind, following her as she slipped between parked cars and jumped up on the curb. He was so focused on where Morgan was going to go next, Nick never noticed a huge puddle of water. He rode right into it, and was forced to slam on the brakes.

Whoosh! Water flew everywhere. And most of it landed on the letterman jacket of Rory "Bonecrusher" Agin, a huge, muscular, tenth-grade football player who was known as much for his bullying as he was for his touchdowns.

Rory's face became twisted with anger. The five hulking football players he was with didn't look too happy either. Rory began smashing his fist angrily into the palm of his hand.

Nick gulped. This was *not* good.

Before Nick could even attempt to apologize, Rory pulled at the younger boy's shirt collar and yanked him off of his bike. Rory's eyes closed to little slits as he thought about how he was going to make Nick pay for what he had done.

"Are you sure we can't talk about this?" Nick gulped. He smiled nervously at Rory.

"I'm going to kill you," Rory snarled. Then he turned to Coleman, who was trying to quietly ride off. "Don't even think of moving, tubby!" Rory told him. "You're next."

Nick's heart pounded wildly with fear as Rory pulled back his arm and got ready to let Nick have it. And then, suddenly, a football whizzed through the air and landed squarely in Rory's stomach. The tenth grader doubled over in pain.

Nick, Coleman, and Elliott looked over in the direction from which the football had been thrown. There stood Morgan, smiling victoriously.

"Good shot, Morgan!" Coleman congratulated her.

Nick didn't say a word. He just picked up his football and rode off as quickly as he could. He didn't want to wait for Rory to stand up again. And he didn't want to thank Morgan for anything, either.

CHAPTER FIVE

MORGAN SAVES THE DAY, AGAIN

The MNFC may have escaped Rory's wrath that time, but it was a sure bet that the angry tenth grader and his cronies would still be looking for them. For most of the school day, the three boys moved cautiously through the hallways, peeking around corners, and trying to bring as little attention as possible to themselves as they made their way from class to class.

But they couldn't avoid Rory forever. Sometime just before fifth period, Morgan grabbed Coleman by the arm, and whispered, "Shh! Rory and his goons are coming!"

Quickly, Morgan pulled Coleman into the nearest bathroom. Elliott and Nick followed close behind.

The boys and Morgan stood silently in hiding as Rory and his buddies turned the corner near the bathroom.

"When I find those squids, they die!" Rory's voice echoed through the halls as he and the other bullies walked by.

As they waited on the other side of the bathroom door, the MNFC guys didn't say a word. They just held their breath and waited for Rory to move on.

Finally, Nick, Elliott, Coleman, and Morgan heard Rory's footsteps walk off into the distance. Now they could relax.

"There's way too much tension in my life," Coleman sighed.

Morgan looked her cousin in the eye. "Okay, Nick. That's twice I've saved you from those idiots," she said. "I want in with you guys!"

Nick shook his head defiantly. "You got Grandpa's football. Isn't that enough?" he demanded.

Morgan rolled her eyes. "Get over it. I don't know why he left the football to me and gave you that jersey. But you guys and Hilary are the only people I know around here."

Elliott turned to Nick. "It *is* kinda cruel to make her hang out with Hilary," he agreed.

Morgan laughed. "Tell me about it," she agreed. "If I have to listen to Hilary recite dialogue from *Clueless* one more time . . . and she always gets it wrong! I *need* to be in the club."

"Wow! I've never been needed before!" Coleman declared.

But Nick seemed unmoved by his cousin's pleas—or by Coleman's slightly bizarre declaration.

"She *can* throw a ball," Elliott coaxed Nick.

"No!" Nick argued. "We don't need a . . ."

"Fine!" Morgan interrupted him. "Then I'll just tell everyone that you like to hang out in the girls' bathroom."

Yikes! The boys looked around in shock. They'd been so worried about getting beaten up by Rory that they hadn't even noticed that Morgan had dragged them into the *girls'* bathroom.

MORGAN SAVES THE DAY, AGAIN

Suddenly Morgan pulled a small disposable camera from her backpack. "Smile!" she told the boys as she snapped a picture of them standing right under the sign showing the picture of a girl that marked every girls' lavatory in the school.

Nick groaned. *Great.* Now his cousin had proof he'd been in the girls' room. Once again, she'd outsmarted him—just as she sometimes outran him, or outthrew him, on the field.

Nobody is going to blackmail me, Nick thought angrily. Especially not Morgan!

Before Nick could say anything, the guys heard a flushing sound coming from one of the stalls. A blond-haired girl walked out of the stall. She took one look at the boys and screamed. Then she ran out of the bathroom.

Someone had seen the MNFC in the

girls' bathroom. Now their reputation was in real danger!

"Let her in the club, Nick!" Coleman pleaded. "Let her in!"

Nick knew he had no choice. "All right," he said finally. "You're in . . . *if* you pass the test.

Coleman looked at Nick. "Test?" he asked curiously.

But Morgan wasn't afraid. "Fine, test me," she agreed confidently.

Nick smiled to himself. He was sure that Morgan would never pass the test he had in mind for her!

Elliott looked from Nick to Morgan and shook his head. Both cousins had the exact same confident grin on their faces. Morgan was every bit as sure of herself as Nick was of himself.

CHAPTER SIX

PUTTING IT TO THE TEST

The very next afternoon, Morgan met the members of the MNFC in the schoolyard. She looked confident and relaxed, if a little annoyed. After all, she was pretty sure that Elliott and Coleman hadn't had to take any test to join the MNFC. Still, if that's what it would take . . .

Nick laughed to himself. He figured his cousin wouldn't be so cocky after she failed his test. That would show her who was the better athlete—*and* who really deserved to get their grandfather's football.

"This is the Quarterback Challenge," Nick told his cousin. "It's a test of accuracy. Elliott's the moving target. You have to hit him nine out of ten times."

Coleman and Elliott—especially Elliott—seemed shocked at the goal Nick had set for Morgan. Not only did it seem impossible, but as far as Eliott was concerned, it might be painful if Morgan actually landed one or two of them.

But Elliott had to believe that Morgan wouldn't be able to hit him. Even Nick probably couldn't pull that one off, and he had the best arm of the three of them.

Morgan remained cool. She took Nick's football and waited for Elliott to drive off on his bike. When Elliott was about twenty yards from Morgan, Nick gave his cousin the signal to begin.

"She's toast," Coleman whispered to Nick. Nick smiled. That was exactly what he was hoping for.

Elliott began riding around in a circle. Morgan reached back and threw the ball at him. *Smack!* The football hit Elliott right in the backpack. His bike wobbled slightly as he shifted his weight.

"Hey, not so hard!" Elliott shouted toward Morgan as he picked up the ball and tossed it back to her.

Morgan shrugged and threw the ball again. This time, she hit Elliott in the thigh.

Time after time, Morgan aimed the ball at Elliott and hit him. Finally, on the ninth throw, she reached back and aimed. It was a good thing Elliott was wearing his helmet. The ball smacked him right in the head. Elliott lost his footing and fell to the ground.

"Aargh!" Elliott moaned. "Are you guys trying to get me killed?"

Nick was as surprised as anyone that his cousin had pulled off such an amazing feat. But he wasn't going to let on.

"All right, Morgan. You passed the first test," he told her. "Phase two, tomorrow."

Coleman looked suspiciously at Nick. "There's a phase two?" he asked him.

Nick smiled at Morgan, as he elbowed Coleman right in the stomach.

By the following afternoon, Nick had come up with a plan that was certain to keep Morgan out of the Monday Night Football Club forever. She was going to

have to beat Coleman at his own game—
guzzling milk shakes. Coleman was a
champion shake chugger. No one in the
whole school could pound down as many
as Coleman could.

As Nick poured out the glasses of milk
shakes, Morgan looked confused. "What
exactly does this have to do with football?"
she asked her cousin, pointing to the
forty multicolored plastic glasses that had
been set up on Nick's kitchen counter.
They were divided into two groups of
twenty. All the glasses were filled to the
top.

"Physical toughness. How much a body
can endure. That's a key ingredient for a
player in the Monday Night Football Club.
Now you've got to shake the 'Slaw," he
explained, pointing toward Coleman.
"Mouths: *ready . . . set . . . DRINK!*"

Morgan and Coleman both grabbed straws into their mouths and began to sip. Each finished their first glass. And then their second. Then their third. But as Morgan reached for her fourth shake, she noticed that Coleman was using two straws to drink his fourth and fifth shakes simultaneously. She drank faster.

Morgan's surprise at Coleman's drinking prowess was not lost on Nick. He grinned. This would all be over soon.

Or would it?

Suddenly, Coleman took a break from his sixth shake.

"What's the matter, 'Slaw? You're not quittin', are you?" Nick asked nervously.

Coleman raised his right index finger, which was his way of asking Nick to just wait one second. "BUURRRP!" Coleman finally let out a huge belch. "Much better," he sighed, as he went on to finish his sixth shake.

After that, Coleman seemed fine. But so did Morgan. She continued to match the 'Slaw shake for shake. Her straw made a slurping noise as she gulped down number seven. Coleman drank number eight straight—without a straw! But Morgan still kept the pace.

And then, somewhere in the middle of shake number sixteen, Coleman stopped drinking. He put his elbows on the counter and clutched his head in pain.

"What're you doing?" Nick shouted at him.

"Brain freeze!!!" Elliott exclaimed hopelessly.

"Aarrggh," Coleman moaned in agony.

Morgan didn't even look at Coleman. That would only serve to interrupt her train of thought. She just kept drinking as quickly as she could. As she finished her sixteenth shake and started sipping her seventeenth, Morgan pounded her fist on the counter with excitement. Coleman had stopped sipping shakes. As soon as she finished this last one, she'd be the winner— and a bona fide member of the MNFC!

Leonardo went into the kitchen and padded over to Coleman. He barked wildly at the boy's feet, but Coleman didn't seem to notice. He was too busy moaning and holding his head and stomach.

Hilary heard the racket and ran into the kitchen. She sat down beside Leonardo and pet the dog, trying to calm his nerves.

"'Slaw, are you okay?" Nick asked finally.

"I haven't seen him like this since he

ate that bucket of nachos," Elliott said with concern. "I think he's gonna . . . FIRE IN THE HOLE!"

Morgan looked up at Coleman's face. It had a strange green hue to it. "Hilary, duck!" Morgan shouted to her older cousin.

But it was too late. Coleman threw up all over the place—and most of it landed on Hilary.

"Aargh! Look at me!" Hilary shouted angrily as she glanced down at her clothing with disgust. There was thrown-up milk shake in her hair, on her shirt, and running down her pant legs. Leonardo was covered with it, too. "Coleman, you're disgusting!"

Morgan moved away from the counter and inched toward her cousin. "Here, Hilary," she said kindly, trying hard not to get too close. "I'll help you get that . . . stuff out of your hair. These guys are totally gross!"

Hilary couldn't have agreed more. She stood up, and kicked Coleman right in the shin. Then she flipped her hair behind her and stormed out, trying to hold on to some of her dignity. Morgan looked at her cousin Nick with disgust. But Nick didn't seem to care.

"Phase three, tomorrow" was all he said. As far as he was concerned, Morgan had not yet earned her way into the MNFC.

Coleman looked from Morgan to Nick, and clutched his head. This war between the cousins was getting out of control. And his head and stomach were the most recent casualties.

• • •

PUTTING IT TO THE TEST

Phase three of the Monday Night Football Club entrance exam was a test of Morgan's football knowledge. All throughout the following school day, Nick threw questions at her about players' records, famous football plays, and strategies. Unfortunately for Nick, Morgan knew just as much about football as he did.

"Okay, one last question," Nick said finally. "In 1926, if the quarterback threw two consecutive incomplete passes, what happened?"

Coleman looked at Nick in amazement. "Did they even have football in 1926?" he whispered to Elliott.

Elliott nodded. Then he turned to Nick. "The guys on *Sports Center* wouldn't even know that," he insisted.

That was the last straw. Morgan finally lost her cool and became angry. This test was *totally* unfair. None of the three original members of the MNFC had had to go through all of this. She decided to give Nick a little taste of his own medicine. "Okay, Nick, what's a play action fake fumblerooskie?" she asked him finally, giving the name of a very old obscure play. Nick stared back at her. He didn't have the foggiest idea what the play was. Morgan smirked and said, "Thirty-three to eight. Eight recovers and bootleg left rocket 80 E.Z."

Coleman, Elliott, and Nick stared at Morgan, dumbfounded. "What language was that?!" Coleman asked finally.

"That's not a play," Nick insisted defensively.

Morgan rolled her eyes and let out a slight, condescending laugh. "Quarterback fakes a hand off to the running back, who fumbles on purpose. The quarterback and running back both dive on the ball. The running back gets up and pretends he has it. The quarterback goes left and rifles it in for a touchdown," Morgan said, smirking.

Whoa! Even Nick had to admit that was an impressive play. He also knew that there was only one place Morgan could have learned a play like that—from their grandfather. That was one of those wacky plays he always seemed to like to reminisce about. Nick wondered quietly why his grandfather had never told *him* about this play action fake fumblerooskie. Maybe his grandfather really had liked Morgan better. Or maybe Nick had been too busy bragging about the more modern plays to listen.

Nick sighed. Anyhow, it didn't matter

if Morgan knew some weird, obscure, ancient play. It was still not enough to get Morgan admitted into the MNFC. The play action fake fumblerooskie was not the question at hand. She was the one who had a quiz to answer. Not Nick.

"Whatever," Nick said finally, trying his best to act unimpressed. "But *I'm* not the one trying to join the MNFC. You are. Do you know the answer to *my* question or what?"

Morgan just shook her head no.

A grin flashed across Nick's face. *It was all over.* Morgan had lost. She was not going to be a member of the Monday Night Football Club.

Nick pumped his fist victoriously in the air. "Yesss!" he exclaimed. "We've got her." He turned to his cousin. "Rules are rules. See ya!!"

Morgan turned to walk away. Then she stopped and stared at her three former friends. "You know, in a couple of years you guys will be begging to hang out with my friends," she assured them, her voice shaking only slightly with anger and disappointment.

"What does she mean by that?" Coleman asked Nick as soon as Morgan was out of earshot.

Nick shrugged. "Who knows. Let's get out of here."

As he walked toward his next class, Nick glanced over his shoulder at Morgan. She looked kind of sad. Suddenly, Nick's victory didn't seem as sweet.

CHAPTER SEVEN

TRAN-SPORT-ED!

On Monday night, Coleman, Elliott, and Nick met in Nick's family room, as they always did. No one mentioned Morgan. Instead, they ate slices of pizza, drank liters of cola, and played their usual pregame make-believe football match.

As always, Nick was Steve Young. He held the football in his left hand and began the game. "The San Francisco

49ers . . . 1994 Super Bowl Champs. Steve Young, hungry to get another championship," he barked, sounding a lot like a TV sportscaster.

Elliott and Coleman gathered around Nick, anxiously awaiting their instructions.

"Okay, deep to the couch, around the lamp, and reverse play," Nick told his pals. "Ready? Go!"

Elliott and Coleman ran the play. Nick watched as they moved around the family room. Then, once Coleman was clear of any lamps, vases, or other breakable objects, Nick let the ball go. Instantly, Coleman dove toward the ball, catching it and falling wildly into the couch. *Bam!* The couch fell over on its back.

Coleman stood up and raised the ball above his head. "Touchdown!" he shouted wildly. "The man, the myth, the 'Slaw!" He bowed to the imaginary stadium of cheering fans.

But Coleman's glory was short-lived. Hilary had just entered the room. Instinctively, Coleman moved as far from her as possible. He didn't know whether this would be the moment Hilary would choose to get back at him for the chocolate milk shake incident.

Hilary laughed at Coleman's obvious discomfort. She stretched her body to its full height and stared at him. Hilary had grown quite a few inches over the summer, and she towered over Coleman—not to mention Nick and Elliott. Coleman gulped.

"Another gathering of the Monday Night *Freak* Club?" Hilary snarled sarcastically at her brother and his friends. "Dad says to try and not break all the furniture." She looked around the room. "Where's Morgan?"

Nick shrugged. "Not in the club. Not here!"

Hilary spotted the raggedy yellow-and-blue wool football jersey thrown lazily over a chair. She walked over, picked it up, and threw it at her brother. "Over *this*?" she asked him. "You're an idiot."

"Game's starting," Elliott called to the others.

That was more than Hilary could bear. She turned and left the room in disgust.

As Nick and his friends watched the football game on TV, Hilary went into the kitchen to call her cousin Morgan. She wanted to convince Morgan to come over and hang out.

But Morgan wasn't in the mood to have another fight with Nick.

"No way, Hil," she told her cousin. "He's such a jerk."

"Whatever," Hilary agreed. "But c'mon. I can't go through another season with just those three. I'm outnumbered. I need another girl here. Besides, you and Nick have been best buds for too long."

Morgan didn't say anything. In the background, Hilary could hear the football game playing on Morgan's TV. She knew from talking to Nick that watching a game alone just wasn't the same as watching it with a group of friends. And Hilary was certain that Morgan felt the same way.

Unfortunately, Morgan could be every bit as stubborn as Nick.

"Maybe I've just outgrown him," Morgan insisted. "I'll talk to you later."

Hilary hung up the phone and sighed.

She couldn't believe that Morgan and Nick weren't speaking over some dumb autographed football. This argument had gone too far.

At the end of the half-time show, Coleman picked up the old woolen jersey Nick's grandfather had left to him. "This thing weighs a ton," he said. "How'd anyone play in it?"

"It can't be that bad. . . ." Nick said.

"Would you guys be quiet?" Elliott interrupted. "The game's on!"

Coleman quickly tossed the jersey over to Nick and hopped into a plush, comfortable chair near the TV.

Nick stared at the jersey. There didn't seem to be anything magical about it. Maybe Elliott was right. Maybe he *had* been daydreaming about being

Charles Woodson. After all, how could an itchy, moth-eaten jersey actually allow you to switch bodies with someone? It was totally impossible. Nick laughed at his own silliness, threw the jersey over his head, and put his arms in the sleeves.

Whooosh! Suddenly there was a wild flash of light. In Nick's mind, everything seemed to be moving in slow motion. His arm slowly switched from its natural color to a clear, see-through vessel. The blood inside had gone from blue and red to water-clear as well, and it moved like gel through the transparent veins. Nick's body began to stretch thinner and thinner. And then, Nick vanished.

"Hey Nick, do you . . ." Coleman turned to ask Nick a question, but his friend had totally disappeared. "Nick?"

TRAN-SPORT-ED!

Elliott turned around. He looked around the room and then stared nervously at Coleman.

Where was Nick?

CHAPTER EIGHT

JIGGIN' ON THE JUMBOTRON

"Yo, Steve! Steve! You're in the game."

Nick looked around him. Suddenly he was sitting on a bench along the sidelines at the Green Bay Packers home stadium. But Nick wasn't sitting with the Packers. Beside him on the bench were members of the San Francisco 49ers.

"C'mon Steve," one of the 49ers said to Nick. "Offense is on the field."

Nick looked around him excitedly.

Obviously the player was talking to Steve Young. Nick couldn't wait to meet him— or at the very least see him from up close. Nick looked up and down the 49ers bench, searching for Young, but he didn't see the famed quarterback anywhere. Nick looked at the other 49ers. They all seemed to be staring right back at Nick. Maybe they were wondering what a kid was doing sitting there on their bench. Nick was wondering that himself.

But that wasn't why the players were staring at him. "Get your butt out there," one of the defensive players called over to Nick.

Nick wasn't quite sure what was going on, but he sure wasn't about to argue with someone that large. Quickly, he put on his helmet (not that he knew where the helmet by his feet had actually come from) and jogged onto the field. He could hear the crowd roaring as he ran to the 50-yard line. It was a sound he didn't think he could describe to anyone ever again. Tens of thousands of people screaming all at one time—and Nick was in the middle of the whole thing. The sound was loud, it was deafening, and it was all aimed at him. Unfortunately, the shouts of the crowd were not encouraging. After all, those people were Green Bay fans. Nick figured it might be really easy for football players to get paranoid—if they didn't have the talent of, say, a Steve Young.

"This is really weird," he muttered quietly to himself as he raced onto the field. But it was kind of exciting, too. Ever since he could remember, Nick had wanted to be part of a major league football game. And now, here he was, in the middle of a real live stadium, with the fans, TV cameras, and pro football players all around him. Nick couldn't wait to be part of the action. Of course, it might help if he knew what position he was supposed to be playing.

The offensive players were already huddled together when Nick reached them. He joined in on the huddle and waited for someone to tell him what to do. After all, these guys were the pros. Unfortunately, the other players were waiting for their quarterback to tell *them* what to do next. And guess who the quarterback was . . .

"Steve, you gonna call a play or what?" one of the players asked Nick. All of the players stared at him. Their eyes were anxiously awaiting his call.

And for the first time, it suddenly hit him. Nick was now inside Steve Young's body. All of these players thought *he* was *Steve Young*!

Nick started to shake. This was impossible. It had to be just like Elliott had told him. This was a dream. A very *cool* dream. But just a dream.

Then, out of the corner of his eye, Nick spotted the JumboTron on the rear wall of the stadium. There was Steve Young, right in the middle of the image. Nick pointed his finger in the air. On the JumboTron, he could see Steve Young doing the exact same thing. Nick put his arm down. So did Steve Young. Nick started wiggling his hips and shaking his arms around, like some sort of psycho Elvis. On the JumboTron, it appeared that Steve Young was the one who had started dancing on the field.

Whoa! Nick thought. This is no

dream—unless you call it a dream come true! Nick was so excited at the prospect of being Steve Young—even if it were just for a little while—that he began doing a victory dance right at the center yard line! To the crowd, that victory dance seemed a little premature, particularly since it was Green Bay who had the lead. But none of that mattered to Nick. He was too excited to care about the score right now.

The crowd roared with laughter. The football announcers were confused. What was Steve Young doing?

"Hey, Steve, save that for the half-time show," one of the announcers laughed.

But the Green Bay Packers didn't find his dancing too laughable. They gritted their teeth angrily and waited for Steve Young to make his move.

The other 49ers weren't laughing either.

"Young! Stop fooling around," one of his teammates ordered.

Nick stopped dancing and thought for a minute. What play would the *real* Steve Young call right about now?

"Okay . . . X waggle, motion right, fake thirty-two dive on three," he told the other players in the most commanding voice he could muster, while trying to hide the unbelievable excitement he was feeling. "Break!"

As the team broke the huddle and walked over to the line of scrimmage, Nick wondered, How did I know that? After all, he'd never laid his eyes on the 49ers playbook.

Regardless of how he'd recalled the play, Nick knew that now he had to play it out. So, he began making the call.

"Blue twenty-eight. Blue thirty-three. Red thirty-two. Hut! Hut! Hut!"

And with that, the play went into motion. The ball was snapped to Nick. He grabbed the ball and stepped into the pocket, ready to make the pass. But before he could release the ball, he was blind-sided and flattened by a huge wall of Green Bay Packers.

"Ugh!" Nick felt the force of a freight train knock him to the ground. The wind blew out of his body, and pain took its place. All the pads in the world couldn't have protected him from the agony he was feeling. He stared in fear at one of the giant football players who had just tackled him to the ground.

"Welcome to Green Bay," the linebacker barked at Nick as he pushed his way off of him.

Nick clutched his side. Obviously, there was more danger to Steve Young's job as quarterback than Nick had realized. Hits from giant linebackers hurt—a lot! Maybe this really *was* more dangerous than playing football while skating on in-line skates or riding your bike down the street.

"This is definitely the most painful dream I've ever had," Nick mumbled as he gasped for air.

But it was no dream. And the proof of that was back in Nick's family room. Coleman and Elliott had searched the house looking for Nick, but he had disappeared. Coleman was so upset he was actually crying! And that was *totally* embarrassing, especially when Morgan walked in the room and caught him in the act.

"Hey, guys," Morgan announced herself, as she swung her backpack over her shoulder and walked into the family room. She spotted Coleman and Elliott right away, but Nick didn't appear to be anywhere in sight.

"They took him!" Coleman shouted incoherently at Morgan, before she could even ask where her cousin had disappeared to. "A flash of light blasted through the room. Gone! It's gotta be aliens!"

Morgan looked at Coleman and shook her head. "Cute, Coleman. Now where's Nick? Really. I want to talk to him."

"I told you. Evaporated!"

Elliott stood and tried to console his panic-stricken pal. "'Slaw, people just don't disappear," he said logically. "He probably heard Morgan coming and he's playing some weird joke."

Morgan sighed. That sounded like something Nick would do.

Coleman stopped crying and considered Elliott's idea for a minute. As usual, what Elliott had said made perfect sense. That was what was so great about having a brainiac friend like Elliott. He brought logic to any situation. "I'm going to kill him!" Coleman announced.

But at that very moment, Nick and the 49ers were already being killed—by the Green Bay Packers. They were four points behind. There were only three minutes left and the 49ers were on their own 40-yard line.

Nick stepped into the huddle. Once again, all eyes were on him. But this time, it didn't feel like fun. It felt like pressure. The toughest pressure Nick had ever been under. The whole team was depending on him, and it was impossible for him to think with all the screaming coming from the crowd. He clutched his side for a second. The pain from the linebacker's pounce was pretty tender, too. He'd better come up with a good play. Nick had no desire to go through being tackled by a bunch of Green Bay Packers again.

"Time for a little Young magic," one of the players said, looking toward Nick.

"They've been reading our offense all night," Nick admitted. "None of our plays are working! I don't know!"

The other players stared at him in disbelief. Was Steve Young actually saying he didn't know what to do? What had happened to the quarterback who was famous league-wide for remaining cool under pressure?

"We have five seconds left and *you don't know*?!" one of Steve's fellow players demanded angrily. Nick gulped. Now even his own teammates seemed to be turning on him. "C'mon. Let's win this thing and go home. Call it, Steve."

Nick thought for a moment. And then, suddenly, he came up with the perfect play. A play that even the 49ers wouldn't have been able to read ahead of time.

"Okay," Nick told his teammates. "Something different. Play action fake fumblerooskie. Thirty-three to eight. Eight recovers and bootleg left rocket 80 E.Z."

The players all looked strangely at their quarterback. This wasn't in their playbook. What was Steve Young talking about?

But Nick knew exactly what he was

talking about. That was the crazy play Morgan had told him. And boy, was he glad she had. It was the only chance the 49ers had of taking this game away from the Packers.

Nick made a mental note to thank Morgan when he got back to being himself again—and to apologize to her for being kind of a jerk about the MNFC. Nick realized that he had been jealous of Morgan, because that autographed football made it seem that she had been so much closer to his grandfather than Nick had. Not to mention the fact that she knew more about football than even Nick did. Nick had to admit that having such a sports-savvy cousin was coming in handy right now.

"Just do it," Nick assured the 49ers offensive line.

Nick may have sounded confident to his teammates, but the truth was he wasn't at all sure that this play would work. After all, he'd never actually seen it work. And even though Morgan had sounded very authoritative when she'd described it to the members of the MNFC, she could have gotten some of the details wrong. And those could be fatal details.

Nick would have been even less convinced that he'd chose the right way for the 49ers to go, had he heard what the TV announcer was saying on the air: "If I were in the crowd now, I'd leave early to beat the traffic."

The 49ers broke the huddle and streamed onto the field. The ball was snapped. Nick grabbed it and pretended to throw. But instead of releasing the ball, he immediately handed it off to the 49ers running back. The running back then fumbled the ball on purpose. The Green Bay fans cheered. They figured the fumble meant the game was over—and Green Bay had won.

But the Green Bay Packers' hometown fans were in for a major surprise!

Nick and the 49ers running back both dove onto the ball at the same exact time. The running back jumped to his feet and ran toward the Green Bay end zone. The Packers followed him, thinking he had the ball. But it was really Nick who had taken hold of the football. Nick turned to his left and rifled the ball down the field into the waiting hands of Jerry Rice, who grabbed it and sprinted for a touchdown!

The crowd was in shock. They'd never seen a play quite like that one before. After all, the last time anyone had ever tried it, there hadn't even been televisions!

But the play was on TV now. And back at Nick's house, Elliott and Coleman were going crazy! They ran around the living room cheering at the top of their lungs. Nick's dad, who was watching in the other room, shouted with delight.

Hilary laughed as she passed by the family room on the way to the kitchen. "Football madness," she remarked to Morgan. "It's everywhere in this house."

Only Morgan stood quietly, staring at the screen. She was awfully surprised by what she had just seen. "That's my play," she muttered. "How would the 49ers know that play?"

Coleman and Elliott were also keenly aware that it had been Morgan's play that had been called. And they were extremely impressed. After all, Steve Young had just used the same little-known trick. And Steve Young was awesome! At this very moment, Nick's cousin Morgan was their hero—even if she was a girl!

"That was Morgan's play," Elliott told Coleman excitedly.

Coleman smiled at Morgan. "We always wanted you to join," he assured her. "It was Nick who didn't."

Morgan nodded. She already knew that was the case. What she didn't know was how Steve Young had learned about the fumblerooskie trick. She'd thought it was one of those old-time plays that only ancient players like her grandfather had known about.

CHAPTER NINE

THE JERSEY'S NO JOKE

Morgan was right. Up until now, hardly anyone had known about the special sneak play her grandfather had once described to her. But now, everyone in the whole country had seen it in action. The play had won the game for the 49ers.

As the final whistle blew, Nick's teammates lifted him onto their shoulders and paraded him around the field. Of course, they had no idea that it was a junior high school boy they were carrying around. They thought it was Steve Young, master quarterback.

But Nick was still Nick at heart. He couldn't hold back the amazing excitement he felt as all of these pro players paraded him around the field like some sort of conquering hero. He waved happily to the crowd, grinned so wide his cheeks hurt, and reached down occasionally to pat some of his fellow 49ers on the back in congratulations. His fellow 49ers! How cool was that?

He also gripped his injured ribs from time to time. The victory sure had been sweet, but it had come with a cost. Nick didn't think he'd ever forget the feeling of all those humongous football players coming down on him in that tackle.

The team hauled Nick into the visitors

locker room and placed him down beside Steve Young's locker. The national sports reporters were already waiting for him. They shoved their microphones in his face and began barking questions at him.

"Steve, how long have you been working on that surprise play?" one reporter asked.

At first, Nick was thrown by all the flashing camera lights and microphones. He didn't know what to say. These press conferences always looked so easy on the other side of the TV.

"The play? It um . . . just came to me," Nick stumbled over his reply. Then he looked into the camera. He searched his mind for a way to let his friends know that it was him and not Steve Young who had called for the play action fake fumblerooskie. Finally, he had an idea. He waved hello at the camera and shouted at the top of his lungs. "Hey! MNFC ROCKS!"

As Nick waved his arm in the air, a fan pulled at his jersey. Nick looked up. Suddenly, he noticed with dismay that his hand had become transparent. Once again, he could see the clear liquid flowing through his veins. This was just like what had happened when he'd changed back from being Charles Woodson. Nick knew his time as Steve Young was coming to an end. He was rapidly changing back to a kid—and he certainly didn't want to do that on national television.

"Uh, I gotta go," he nervously told the reporters as he ran away from the lights and the cameras. "Sorry."

Nick ran down the hall of the locker room as quickly as he could. He wanted to get as far from the reporters and the 49ers as he possibly could. He searched for a private corner where he could switch back into himself. But before he could find a quiet place to disappear, Jerry Rice grabbed him from behind.

"Way to go, Stevie boy!" Jerry congratulated Nick. "I knew you'd find me."

Nick struggled to break Jerry's hold on him. But the wide receiver had a tight grip.

"Er? Jerry Rice?" Nick asked.

"Yeah, buddy," Jerry affirmed. "Your man with the hands."

Jerry lifted Nick higher off the ground. "Hey, Steve," he asked. "Are you losing weight?"

Nick looked down. He sure *was* losing weight—not to mention whole body parts! Both of his legs were beginning to stretch out and disappear! Quickly he squirmed from Jerry Rice's arms and ran off down the long hallway leading away from the locker room.

"You gotta eat more, man!" Jerry yelled after him. "We're going all the way! Super Bowl 2001!"

Suddenly everything seemed to be going in slow motion. Nick looked at his right hand. It was gone. So was his arm. "This can't be good," he murmured.

Quickly Nick used his left hand to lift off his 49ers jersey to check and see if his chest and stomach were still there. They were, but not for long. Within seconds, Nick had completely disappeared from the 49ers locker room.

CHAPTER TEN

A MESSAGE FROM STEVE YOUNG

The next thing Nick knew, he was back in his own family room. And instead of Steve Young's uniform, he found himself once again wearing the itchy yellow-and-blue football jersey his grandfather had left to him. He whipped off the jersey and looked at his hands and arms. Yep, everything was right back in place.

Nick looked down at the jersey and smiled. Now he knew why his grandfather had left the jersey to him. The shirt was magical. And more important, it was able to give Nick a firsthand view of what it felt like to be a real sports star. Nick rubbed his sore ribs. He grinned and thought of his grandfather. The old man had been right. Being a sports hero obviously took a lot more effort than just being able to smile at the camera and hold up a new box of cereal. It took brains, talent, and a lot of hard work—not to mention strength! Nick knew he had a lot to learn, and obviously his grandfather had been determined to teach him his lessons—even if he couldn't be there to do it himself.

Having the magic jersey left to him had been an honor, not a rip-off. Nick was embarrassed at how he had been thinking. And, he suddenly felt pretty bad about the way he had been treating Morgan ever since his grandfather's trunk had arrived at his house.

"Nick! Where have you been?" Elliott demanded as he turned to see Nick standing in the doorway. "They called Morgan's play to win the game!"

"No, it was me!" Nick insisted. "*I* was Steve Young. I called Morgan's play!"

Morgan rolled her eyes. Nick was obviously taking this pretend quarterback thing a little too far.

"Young's on the news," she told him, as she pointed to the screen. "And he doesn't look anything like you, Nick."

Nick looked up at the screen. The network was showing the taped interview he had just given. Sure enough, there was Steve Young, in the locker room, talking to reporters. Nick smiled. He knew exactly what was going to be said at this interview. After all, he'd been there—inside Steve Young's body.

"The play, it um . . . just came to me," Steve Young was saying. Then he looked into the camera and shouted, "MNFC ROCKS!!!"

Elliott, Coleman, and Morgan looked at each other with complete surprise.

"What?!" Elliott exclaimed.

"Huh?" Coleman added.

"Did you hear that?" Morgan asked the others.

Nick smiled triumphantly. "See! It was me!!!" he declared.

Coleman backed nervously away from Nick. "You . . . you . . . really were Steve Young?"

Nick nodded. "I was Steve Young. How cool is that?"

Coleman looked more petrified than impressed. "I wanna go home. I wanna go home now," he whimpered.

Morgan and Nick looked at the jersey, which was lying in a heap on the floor.

"No way!" they both said at once.

Elliott was sure the jersey was responsible for the switch. "It had to be that," he told the others.

Nick picked up the jersey and tossed it over to Elliott. Elliott studied the jersey for a minute to see if there were any clues to how it might work.

Coleman was less scientific about the whole thing. He just wanted to get as far from this magic football jersey as was humanly possible.

Nick walked over to Morgan and looked her in the eye. "Morgan, the 49ers would have lost without you. It was your play," he admitted. "So welcome to the Monday Night Football Club."

"Thanks, Nick," Morgan replied gratefully. "Grandpa told me that play. He also told me it's good sportsmanship to share." Morgan reached into her backpack and pulled out the autographed Packers' '67 football. Quietly, she handed it to her cousin.

Nick stared at the ball for a minute. "Really?" he asked Morgan.

Morgan nodded and smiled at Nick. His friendship meant more than the ball did. And maybe that was the lesson her grandfather had wanted her to learn all along.

Nick was so excited that he reached over to hug Morgan. Then he realized the guys were staring at him. How embarrassing! Quickly he raised his hand for a high five, and she did, too.

Elliott looked inside the sleeves of the

jersey. He ran his hands over the letter H that was sewn onto the front. "It's just an old jersey," he declared.

Morgan grabbed the sweater from his hands and put it on. Then she waited to see what would happen. There was no flash of light. And she didn't disappear.

"Right now, it's just making me a fashion victim!" Morgan declared.

Nick tossed the autographed Packers ball at Morgan. She pulled back and tossed it toward Coleman. But instead of gently lobbing through the air, the ball moved like a bullet. Coleman ducked. He didn't even want to *try* to catch that ball!

That was a smart move on Coleman's part.

CRASH! The ball went straight through the family room window and out into the backyard.

"Whoa!" Nick exclaimed.

"Yeow!" Elliott seconded.

Morgan looked at her hands in amazement. "How'd I do that?" she wondered.

But there was no time to think about that now. Nick's dad had already run into the room. And he wasn't happy.

"Did you guys break a window?" he demanded.

Coleman, Nick, and Elliott stared at the jersey Morgan was wearing. They knew Nick's father wouldn't believe it even if they told him. That jersey *definitely* had some sort of magical power to it.

The question was, where was it going to take them next?

FROM THE JERSEY #2
NO GIRLY-GIRLS ALLOWED!

CHAPTER ONE

SPLASHDOWN!

Morgan adjusted her bike helmet and watched as her cousin Nick sped off along the dirt road on his BMX bike. Nick picked up speed as he pedaled, eventually reaching the top of the hill. Then he took off and flew into the sky.

"Look at me! I'm an air god!" he screamed as he leaped.

Not to be outdone, Nick's buddy, Coleman, picked up speed, leaping off the mound close behind Nick. "Superman!" Coleman shouted as he took off from the hill, lifted his feet off his bike pedals and lay flat across the frame of the bike. He flew through the air looking a lot like a flying super hero.

Morgan, the only girl in the group of BMX daredevils, was not the kind of female who would be outdone by the guys. She was every bit as much of a daredevil as they were—in fact, maybe even more so. She quickly picked up speed, and pedaled up to the top of an even higher hill.

"GRAVITY SHATTERS!" she bellowed as she shot her bike straight up in the air.

By the time Morgan hit the ground, Coleman and Nick were already off on a new BMX track, climbing ever higher past mud puddles and through thick dirt. Morgan picked up the pace to join them.

Morgan, Coleman, and Nick were so engrossed in their race to the top of the hill that they hardly even noticed that their buddy Elliott—who was not exactly known for his athletic prowess—was trailing far behind.

Nick and Morgan were cousins. They'd been buddies ever since they were babies. But that didn't keep them from competing with each other every chance they got. Like now. Nick hit the top of the the highest hill at the dirt BMX track, and soared off doing a 360 spin on his bike before landing below. "Eat my dust!" he called up to Morgan.

No problem. Morgan followed her cousin's lead, flew off the top of the hill, and did a 360 as well.

"Show-offs," Coleman called down to both of his buddies as he rode, leaping off the hill to join them. Elliott followed behind, biking downhill instead of leaping. There was no way he was going to try a 360 spin in the air. Elliott was way too cautious for that.

"Check it out," Nick told his pals as soon as they were all gathered at the foot of the hill. He leaned forward in his seat, and began pedaling his bike as hard as possible, gaining all the speed he could. "I'm gonna break the record," he vowed as he looked down at the mud puddle below. Nick, Morgan, and Coleman often had contests to see who could jump over the largest mud puddle without landing in the thick, gooey stuff.

Morgan looked at the puddle. It was huge. She wasn't so sure Nick could clear it. But Nick seemed absolutely positive that he could. He leaped off the hill, soared through the air, and totally cleared the mud puddle. But his joy was extremely short-lived. When Nick's bike did finally hit land, it came down smack in the middle of an even bigger mud puddle than the one he'd tried to jump.

The bike plopped into the mud pile with a huge force. Mud rocketed all over the place. The shock caused Nick to lose his bearings. He fell off his bike and right into the mud.

A group of teenage girls and their boyfriends gathered around Nick as he sat up and wiped the thick black-brown sludge from his face. The girls giggled and their boyfriends laughed hysterically. Nick could feel his face turning red beneath the dark mud mask. He looked sheepishly to his friends for help.

"What are they laughing at?" Nick moaned with embarrassment as Morgan,

Elliott, and Coleman waded into the mud and helped Nick to his feet.

"Don't worry about them. We know we're cool," Morgan assured her cousin as she righted his bike and pulled it onto firmer ground.

"Yeah, who needs 'em?" Coleman agreed.

"I don't care what those girls think," Elliott added.

"Me neither," Nick said. But he didn't sound as convincing as the others had. After all, they hadn't been the ones the girls had been laughing at. And not just any girls—older girls, and their boyfriends. Nick had just looked like a total jerk in front of all of them!

"Exactly," Morgan told the guys. "My opinion is the only one that matters."

Nick, Coleman, and Elliott just stared at Morgan. Was she serious?

"Kidding," she assured the guys as she raised her hand for a high five.

As Nick slapped his cousin's hand, he gave her a wink of gratitude. Her joke had definitely lightened the situation. Nick was really glad Morgan had moved to town from Chicago. And he was thrilled that she liked hanging around with him and his buds. It certainly wasn't every girl who liked to sit around on Monday nights and watch football games. But Morgan was a welcome addition to the Monday Night Football Club (or MNFC, for short)—of which Nick, Coleman, and Elliott were the only other members. Nick had formed the club so he and his friends could be guaranteed that they would watch all the Monday Night Football games, together. They met Mondays at Nick's house, ate pizza, drank Coke, and watched the game.

If Morgan had been a real girly-girl, the kind who only care about reading fan magazines, wearing makeup, and shopping at the mall for hours, it would have been hard for Nick and her to have stayed so close. But Morgan seemed to like everything the guys did. That made it easy for Nick and her to hang out together.

Besides, if Nick really wanted to admit it, he would have to say that Morgan was at least as good an athlete as he was. Maybe even better at some sports. Take soccer. She'd only been at the local junior high for a few months, and already Morgan was the lead scorer on the varsity team. Nick didn't know anyone—girl or guy—who could claim something like that.

All of that made it easy for Nick to trust

Morgan with the MNFC's biggest secret—
a magic football jersey that had been left to
Nick by his grandfather when he died.

At first Nick had not been too thrilled
to have been willed a ratty, old, scratchy
woolen football jersey. But then he had
discovered the secret of the magic jersey:
If you put the jersey on at just the right
time, you became a famous sports star.
The trouble was, you never knew when
the right time was.

Nick himself had already entered the
bodies of football players Charles
Woodson and Steve Young. Morgan had
tried on the same jersey, and although she
hadn't actually turned into a pro player,
she'd discovered a strength in her throwing arm that she had never had before.
(She probably shouldn't have used it inside Nick's house, however. The MNFC

was still paying Nick's dad back for the family room window she'd broken.)

Being inside a pro sports player's body was just about the most amazing experience any sports fan could imagine. But it was also a huge responsibility to that player's teammates. After all, they never knew it was really just a kid inside there. Only the biggest sports fans could be trusted with a job like that. And Nick's cousin Morgan was one of them.

By the time Nick climbed back on his bike, Morgan was already well on the way up another hill on the BMX trail. She turned and gave Nick a look that dared him to beat her to the top. Nick pedaled harder. He couldn't let his cousin beat him! Not this time, anyway.

THE JERSEY

Morgan has a huge crush on a fellow soccer player. She decides the only way for her to win his affections is to make him believe he is a better player than she is.

But everything changes when she puts on the jersey and becomes Cobi Jones!

Find out how Morgan scores big in . . .

THE JERSEY #2
No Girly-Girls Allowed!

AVAILABLE JULY 2000

Check out *The Jersey* on Disney Channel

© Disney